THE LOST BLACKSMITH GENERAL

Bhargava Reddy Chinthareddy

ISBN 978-93-5610-461-7
© Bhargava Reddy Chinthareddy 2022
Published in India 2022 by Pencil

A brand of
One Point Six Technologies Pvt. Ltd.
123, Building J2, Shram Seva Premises,
Wadala Truck Terminal, Wadala (E)
Mumbai 400037, Maharashtra, INDIA
E connect@thepencilapp.com
W www.thepencilapp.com

DISCLAIMER: *This is a work of fiction. Names, characters, places, events and incidents are the products of the author's imagination. The opinions expressed in this book do not seek to reflect the views of the Publisher.*

Author biography

This is my first and foremost book that I ever written and I think it's a great one. I don't know when I'll write a next one. I never says anything like I like to write books or anything because most of the people know that's a lie. so I will say that if you like my book please read my other books that I write in future. I would like to thank you for reading my book.

CONTENTS

Foreword

I would like to thank pencil publication and readers for giving me a such wonderful oppurtinity. The story was completely fictional and not based on anyone. this story is not to hurt any religion or nation or anything. thanks for showing your interest and reading this book. have a great time...

Preface

The story of a mighty general who lost everything in his life and lives alone in wild in search of happiness till his last breath. Did the general had a happy ending or a sad ending.

The empire

Once there was a emperor in an empire that goes by name Heavens land. Which consists of some small kingdoms. There empire was very prosperous under the emperor rule. The emperor never wages a war against any other empires even though he can win against them but if any empire wages war against him empire he will completely defeat them and make their under his ruling. The emperor father named him as Hercules. So that he can also become a great fighter like Hercules in the legends. The emperor was a great man of nature and a mighty strong warrior as Hercules. The emperor studied in a small academy while hiding his identity as royalty to understand the commoners problems. Under the emperor there was a strong army and great wise people to make the empire flourish so well in all the sectors like marketing, cropping, law enforcing and some others. In the empire there were some academies that teach people art, fighting and some others. Of all the academies in the empire Twin judgement academy, Snow lotus academy, Sun fire academy are the top academies in the empire. The responsible authority person selects the persons from academies to serve for the empire and fight for the empire in their respective department. Under the emperor there was a mighty and great war strategist general. The name of the general was Advay and he was self respected and upright person. The emperor and the general both studies in same academy and both of them are good friends. The whole empire known by his title "The Blood Knight" which was not given by the emperor for his achievements but by the soldiers who fight alongside him in war. The general fight in the war like a lion that has been starving for a few days in which means he directly jumps into the enemy front lines attack and disrupts their formations and make them confused which leads for his victory. By the time of end of the day his armor was stained red by enemies blood so the soldiers call him the blood knight. He was the youngest general in the empire. Under the general there are 250 soldier who are personally trained by himself and are placed in different position based on their skills. For war 230 soldiers and the remaining 20 soldiers are spies and assassins. The general never cares about nobility or having high status in the empire. Once in a war the emperor bestowed a nobility status to the general. He kindly rejected the emperor and asked the emperor a training ground and small residential area for soldiers under me. The emperor agreed and gave the general some and promoted his battalion. After that the general requested the emperor that he will directly report and take orders directly from the emperor and the emperor agreed while some nobles are against it. Due to that most of the noble dislike him. Likewise in the same way the general dislikes some nobles saying they are nobles and commoners are not like them. Due to their arrogance the general never take a single noble under him even the emperor himself orders him to train nobles lineage he kindly rejected the requests.

The emperor

The emperor has two wives and two princes and one princess. The first wife was a well dignified and royalty woman of neighbouring country and her name was Kahika. She respects everyone in a good manner. She is the first wife of the emperor and she was a great beauty. she has a son and a daughter. Both of them are well mannered ones and the princess is a good strategist and her name was Vritika. The first prince was good at strategy and fighting and his name was Roshan. The second wife was a noble's daughter who despise commoners and her name was Asmita. She always looks down on commoners and treat them as animals due to her nobility. She has a son. He was also despise commoners like his mother and his name was Tushar. Due to their royal status none of the commoners place a complaint against them to the emperor or law enforcement. One day when she was passing by on the road she ordered her knights to hit a soldier in-front of her carriage who is crossing the road while helping an elder. The soldier that she hurted was under the general's command. The general come to know what happened to the soldier from his spies. He went to the emperor hall and asked the emperor to call his second wife to the hall. The emperor immediately summoned her to the hall. As soon as she entered the hall the general slapped her and warned all the people "If anyone ever touches a person under my command that is the last day of their life even if the emperor himself came I won't spare any." with a strong temperament and loud voice. From that day onwards she hold a grudge against the general. She made her son to hold a grudge against the general like her. He was good at literature and swords.

The general

The general had a beautiful wife and during giving birth to a girl she expired. He named her as Dayita. The girl was raised by the solders families under his command. She was a beautiful person like her mother. She was good at literature and war. The general trained her like a normal solder as she was good at literature. The emperor treats her as his daughter and brought her an admission to the Twin Judgement academy along with her daughter. At first the general disagreed to send her daughter to that academy but the emperor convinced him. He send her daughter to the academy along with the princess Vritika. Both of them joined in the department of literature and war strategies.

Nobles conspiracy

A few days later all the nobles along with Asmita planned a strategy to kill the general and his troops without anyone knowing it. They implemented their plan by making a scout to inform the emperor a wrong number of soldier of Northern snow empire are waiting for an attack and their number is around 2500. As soon as the emperor heard the news he immediately ordered the general of the solder to take a 3000 solders and attack their base then Asmita interfered and asked the emperor to send send general Advay and his troops to attack. Even if the enemy solders are strong he will definitely finishes them and there is nothing to worry. The emperor think it for a minute and ordered general Advay and his troops to attack the enemy base. The general asked the emperor for an extra reinforcement of about 500 elite solders to be under his command on this mission in case if something goes wrong there my be inevitable battle between the two empires.

The war

The general went to the war along with his solders and 500 elite solders. By the end of the day they reached near the enemy camp base. In night the solders are guarding their base the general send two messenger birds in two directions one is towards the emperor and the other is towards the enemy base. The message that send to the emperor was "We reached near the enemy base and we will attack tomorrow morning.". The message that he sent towards the enemy base was "Send me details of exact solders number including their rankings and weaponry". He got two messengers in return one was from empire written as "The nobles conspired and planned all for your death and Asmita was main the one". The other one was enemy base written that "10 generals, 5 commanders, 17985 solders (2000 horse riders, 2000 archers, 1500 spearmen, 12485 swordman)". Then the general in return send a messenger bird to enemy base written in that "kill the generals and commanders silently and come to me". The general send another messenger bird to the empire written in that " If I came back alive that is your death day". As soon as Asmita received the message she ordered to kill the scout. The spy under the general finished his activity and returned to the general before sunrise. Without the commanders and generals the enemies lost the war. The general and his solders along with 200 elite solders returned to the empire. The general stated everything except the nobles conspiracy to the emperor. The emperor angrily ordered the solders to summon the scout. The solders went to summon the scout returned and said that the scout was escaped from the empire.

The banquet

As for the victory of the general the emperor hold a banquet for victory celebrations. All the nobles, higher officials of the empire attended the banquet. The emperor awarded the general with some money. The banquet went very well and in the middle of the banquet Roshan returned from his mother's nation who went on a tour. As soon as he entered the banquet hall the emperor stated that he is going to be the next emperor of the empire. After the banquet the emperor asked the general how did they managed to survive in that battle. The general said that "Who is the one that made the weaponry and armors for my solders." with a smile. Then the general left the banquet saying his wishes to the emperor. The general returned to the barracks and shared the money that the emperor gave him equally to all his solders. The following day night the general celebrated their victory with all his solders in his training grounds.

Dayita's death

After the banquet a week has passed and a report was arrived for general saying that his daughter was killed by a wild animal during training. After reading that the general felt very angered and calmed himself and asked one of his men to go to the academy to investigate about the incident in secrecy. The general performed the after processes of died Dayita. After two days one of his spies returned to the barracks with severe wounds on her body. The general ordered his men to treat her immediately and his men take her to treatment. After two day she recovered and told the general that the death of Dayita was planned in before by Tushar and academy vice dean. The general was enraged in anger and ordered his solders for an attack on the academy. As all the solders preparing for attack on the academy the solder that general sent to the academy to investigate returned with princess Vritika. Vritika requested the general to talk in privacy and general take her to his study room.

Vritika explained everything that happened in the academy and the matter is same as his spy said. The general asked Vritika to go to the palace and wait for him in the palace. Sometime after Vritika left the general ordered all his solders to attack the academy. When the generals solders are about to reach the academy the dean of the academy got the news and he himself went to the front door to greet the general. As soon as the dean saw the general the dean asked for the generals visits to his academy. The general said that "To seek justice for his daughters death" with a angry voice. As the dean doesn't know about the vice dean conspiracy the dean asked the general what happened.

The general told everything to the dean and as soon as the dean heard everything he ordered the academy enforcement to summon vice dean here. The enforcement team went and summoned the vice dean. As soon as the vice dean saw the general he was tensed and the dean asked the vice dean about the conspiracy. The vice dean said nothing and remained silent. The general who was controlling his anger get frustrated and beheaded the vice dean and went back to his barracks with his solders. The general sent a challenge to the Asmita's father for a which is 3 round's bout. For each round that Asmita's father loses one of his lineage dies and if the general loses a single bout they can have his life. But if incase Asmita's father loses all 3 bouts then he will be deprived from his noble status.

The bout

As soon as Asmita father got the news about the bout he asked the emperor as he wasn't a he would like to substitute him with his son and two other knights as all the empire knows about general's achievements in war. The emperor relayed the same to the general. The replied to the emperor word by saying that he will enter the bout without any armor and one person from him for one round and no back of at any round of the bout. Asmita's father accepted for the generals conditions. Asmita's father prepared two finest warriors in the empire for the bout.

The day for the bout has arrived. The emperor, nobles, knights and several people came to the coliseum to watch the bout. Soon the bout started and the general entered the arena with a single sword on his waist. Asmita's father men entered the arena with heavy armor and a spear. The emperor loudly said start the bout.

As soon as the bout started the knight jumped forward and attacked the general with his spear and the general evaded that attack. Like that around 40 moves have been exchanged and the general turned aside while the knight is trying to stab the general with his spear. As the general waiting for an opportunity he slide his sword along with the knight spear. As the general's sword is about to reach the knight hand he leaves the spear and went a step back and thus concluded the first bout. The emperor announced the first bout results as general's win.

For the second bout Asmita's father sent the second Knight. The emperor as the general does he want to take some rest. The general said and he want to continue the bout then the emperor announced the start of the second bout. As soon as the bout started the knight jumped forward and attacked the general with his sword and the general evaded that attack. Like that around 60 moves have been exchanged and the general defended himself while the knight is trying to attack the general with his sword. As the general waiting for an opportunity he slide his sword along with the knight sword. As the general's sword is about to reach the knight sword middle the general applied more force and damaged the knight sword. Thus concluded the second bout and the emperor announced the second bout results as general's win.

For the third bout Asmita's brother went the arena. The emperor as the general does he want to take some rest. The general said and he want to continue the bout then the emperor announced the start of the third bout. As soon as the bout started the knight jumped forward and attacked the general with his sword and the general evaded that attack. Like that around 50 moves have been exchanged and the general defended himself while he was trying to attack him with his sword. The general waiting for an opportunity then he applied a strong force with his sword and damaged the Asmita's brother sword and be headed him with a single stroke. Thus concluded the third bout and Asmita asked the why did he beheaded her brother in a loud angry voice.

The emperor stopped her and asked the general the same thing. The general asked Vritika to explain everything to the emperor and then the general explained the conspiracy of the noble by showing the scout who gave the emperor false information of the enemy soldiers in the previous battle. The emperor asked the general how did he caught the scout. The general replied to the emperor words by saying that one of his spies caught him in severe wounded state and treated him. After completing his words the asked his men to brought a box. As per the general's command his solder brought the box. In side the box there was a sword and general unsheathed the sword and said that is was a presentation to Vritika by forcefully throwing at Tushar.

The emperor asked the general why did he killed Tushar. The general said that it wasn't revenge or anything it was Asmita's and she has to feel the same pain karma like me along with her father. After that the general asked the emperor to take a close look at that sword. The emperor saw the sword closely and backed with surprised and asked Vritika to show her sword to him then Vritika asked the emperor why. The emperor said that he will tell her that later and the emperor take a good look at her sword and surprised. The emperor said that you can leave the arena then the general said I'm just not leaving the arena, I'm leaving the empire. The emperor requested the general to stay then Asmita interrupted the general. As soon as she interrupted the emperor, the emperor ordered his men to lock her in underground dungeon for 10years. The general say sorry for rejecting him and left the empire. Before the general leaving the arena he promised the emperor that he'll return when his karma meets. The general said to Vritika that the sword in her hand is winter moon and the other one on the stage is summer sun and left the arena. At that day evening when the emperor is alone in his room then Vritika entered the room and asked the emperor about the sword. The emperor showed her his sword and there was a emblem on that sword same as on her sword. Vritika asked about the emblem on the sword then the emperor said that the sword was given by his father. His father said that when given he was giving the emperor he said if you ever see a person holding the same sword with same emblem on it other than royalty never ever provoke them by any reason. Then Vritika asked the emperor who was the one that make the sword. The emperor said that he doesn't know either and his father didn't say the persons name but said that their family is great blacksmiths and warriors. At the meantime the emperor received a messenger bird from the general. In that message it's written as "The one who made the winter moon and summer sun was him". The emperor disposed the message by turning it into ashes without telling Vritika.

The blacksmith general

On the same day night the general in his room drinking and thinking of his past. When he was a kid his father teaches him a blacksmith technique which is unique to his family but the general never shows interest in blacksmith technique. One day his father saw him practising sword then his father said "if you learns the blacksmith technique then I will teach you a strong sword technique." as soon as the general heard his father words he got excited and agreed to his father. From the next day the general started learning smithy.

One day at night the emperor's father came to the general's father in person without any security and asked the general's father to make a sword for his son. The general's father said that he was a kid now and why do he need a sword right now. The emperor father said I will give him that sword when he attends the academy then the general's father agreed but on one condition that he never reveals his name. The general was hearing their conversation in secrecy. The next day the general asked his why did he put that condition to hide his identity when he is making the sword. General's father give a smile to general question and replied that with fame and status there will be a great responsibility and enmity. If you can protect your loved one's and empire then it's a great achievement in your life.

After learning the smithy technique his father showed a emblem and said that for every sword or armor you make place the emblem on it. The emblem shouldn't be eye catching and should be seen on keen observation by anyone. After a few days the general's father teaches him sword technique. After the general turned 15 years his father sent him to academy for study. In the academy the general studied war strategies and sword arts like the emperor. As both of them are in same departments and became good friends helping each other. In the academy the emperor knows that the general was a blacksmith. After graduating from the academy the general joined the army and formed his own regiment. The general himself prepared the armors and swords for his regiment.

Disband of regiment

The next day after the bout the general went to the emperor and requested for a private talk. The emperor call-off all the meetings for that day and entered his personal living room. The general summoned all his spies in emperor hall to wait outside the emperor living room with another 8 people that he brought along with him to the emperor hall. After entering the room the general asked the emperor to summon Roshan and Vritika to there. The emperor ordered his knights to summon both of them. After sometime they both entered the room and the general said that he is leaving the country. The emperor asked him to stay but he kindly rejected and said that he is going to disband his regiment. The emperor stayed calmly for a minute and asked the general does he would like to put them under some general or something. The general shakes his head as a no and asked the emperor to revoke his regiment achievements, rankings and other details from records. The emperor asked the general "can I have a copy of the records." the general agreed to emperor but on one condition that he never let the records to other hands except royals. The emperor agreed to the general's condition. The spies that are waiting outside the emperor room send a message to the barracks about the disband of the regiment by general. The emperor announced a 1000gold coins for each member under his team and his knight to summon financial adviser to his room. After that the general called his spies and 8 members out side the room to get-in. All the 12 members entered the room and the general revealed the identities of his 4 spies. All of them apologized to the emperor and asked for his forgiveness for not telling in before.

The general said about the disband of his regiment asked them are they willing to work under the emperor. They rejected and said that they will never work under anyone other than the general. After that the general said that he trained 4 knights under him who likes to work under prince Roshan and introduced them to the prince. After that the general introduced the other 4 knights who would like to work under princess Vritika. Vritika and Roshan both of them thanked the general for giving them knights. The general asked the 12 of them to wait outside the room and they left the room. The general and others talked for about an hour. Before leaving the room the general said to Vritika that he was the one who made both that swords and asked her to take care of the both swords. Vritika said that she will take good care of them.

After that the emperor said that he will drop the general outside the palace and went with the general outside the palace. As soon as the general exited the palace with the emperor, the solders under the general was waiting for him. After seeing them general understand that the disband of regiment news was sent to them. The general asked all of them would they like to work under the emperor. All of them said no in a monotone. At the same time financial advisor of the empire came with some bags containing 1000gold coins each. The emperor ordered his knights to distribute each solder under the general a bag and the knights distributed the bags. After that the general asked all his solders to do small businesses all around the empire and returned the residential area and barracks to the emperor for the empire. After that the solders under the general asked the emperor with empire solders armors and swords about 500 sets for tomorrow one day. The emperor asked them for what purpose the they said that they want to pledge their loyalty to the general with their life partners. The emperor agreed to them and ordered his knights to prepare the armors and swords. On the next following day the general solders along with their life partners gathered in their barracks and called the general to come there. After the general entered the barracks they pledged their loyalty to the general by drawing their swords along with their life partners and pointing the swords towards the sky by vowing to the heavens that they will never work for anyone other than general and are always awaits for the general's return.

Life in forest

Before going into the forest the general prepared some camping tools to make his living in the forest for some days. After a few days of entering the forest the general made a wooden house for himself in the forest with a small backyard near a river. The general daily went to forest to collect some fruits or meat to eat. Most of the time time he collects only fruits and occasionally hunt monsters. For most of the times he does fishing in a manner that no one fishes. Whenever he catches a fish he will throw it back to the river again. Occasionally catches the fishes for eating purpose. Sometimes he wanders all the forest and if he meet any traveler's he ask them about happenings in the empire. While travelling with the traveler's if he saw any bandits he will beat them to pulp and ask the traveler's to hand over them to enforcement team and help them to reach out the forest safely. Sometimes he saw his solders while wandering the forest as some of them are settled as merchants. Whenever he meets them he take them to his house and have a chat with them. Before sending them he ask them about the well-being of the others. After that he help them to leave the forest.

A few years passed and one day the general saw a academy student was chased by a lion. To help the student the general fought with the lion and is seriously injured. The general asked the student to take him to his house as it was near to that area. The student carried the general to his house and after reaching the house the general asked the student does he have some bandages and ointments. The student took out some bandages and ointments from his bag and applied to the general wound. After that the general rested for a night and asked the student for his details. The student said that his name was Vivaan and thanked the general for saving his life. After sometime the student is preparing to leave then the general saw the sword summer sun is with the student. The general asked him where did he get that sword and the student said that he brought in a store. Then the general asked who is Vritika to you and the student said "I can't reply to that" please forgive me. The general asked who is Roshan to you and the student said the same and in return the student asked the general how does he knows the sword. The general said that he was Advay with a smile. As soon as the student hear that he said that he was the current emperor Roshan's son. Then the general teaches him his sword techniques for about half a year and after that one day general passed away due injuries caused during his fight with the lion. After the general passed away Vivaan take the general's body to the empire and informed to all the solders under him previously. After a day most of his solders attended there and cremated the general like royal.

Dedication

I dedicate this book to the Indian army, navy and air force who dedicate their lives for the country. The persons who are fighting for their homeland are real heroes. Jai Hind!

End matter

I would like to thank everyone for selecting this book and reading it. This is my first book and hope everyone took a liking to it. please forgive me id any mistakes are in it and if you have any suggestions for me send at bhargavareddychintareddy@gmail.com. Thank you.